THE DOG WHO SAVED SANTA

True Kelley

HOLIDAY HOUSE / New York

The text typeface is Pink Martini.
The artwork for this book was created with acrylics,
pen and ink, watercolors, and colored pencils.
www.holidayhouse.com
First Edition
1 3 5 7 9 10 8 6 4 2
Library of Congress Cataloging-in-Publication Data
Kelley, True.
The dog who saved Santa / by True Kelley. – 1st ed.
p. cm.
Summary: With the help of his take-charge dog Rodney
and a self-help video, young Santa Claus mends his lazy
and irresponsible ways.
ISBN-13: 978-0-8234-2120-6 (hardcover)
[1. Santa Claus—Fiction. 2. Dogs—Fiction. 3. Humorous
stories.] I. Title.
PZ7.K2824Do 2008
[E]—dc22
2007041180

For Jada and Steve
with thanks to Regina Griffin

The head elf was frantic. 'Twas the night before Christmas, and Santa's elves were swamped.

Even Santa's dog, Rodney, was put to work.
Everyone was working way too hard . . .

except Santa.

Young Santa was dozing off on the couch,
watching TV, and eating fruitcake.
He was no help at all to the elves and Rodney.

Once in a while Santa got up
to go to the refrigerator.
But he was pretty useless.

Santa was a slacker.

The elves and Rodney filled Santa's sack.
They hitched up the reindeer to the sleigh.

They loaded the toys.
They loaded Santa.

Just in case of trouble, Rodney thought he'd better go along.

Off they flew across the starry sky!

Santa found the view mildly interesting.
"Bow WOW!" said Rodney.

They landed on the first roof,
and Santa slid down the chimney.

There were a lot of stockings that needed filling. That looked like WORK to Santa. He sat down to think about how hard it might be and polished off all the cookies and milk.

Then Santa stood up with a sigh. He pulled out a small, random toy and left it on the table.

He put his finger beside his nose and zipped up the chimney.
That was the most fun part for Santa.

When Santa got back in the sleigh, Rodney saw that he looked
tired already. It would be a LONG night.

"ROOF!" said Rodney as he skillfully landed the sleigh on the second roof.

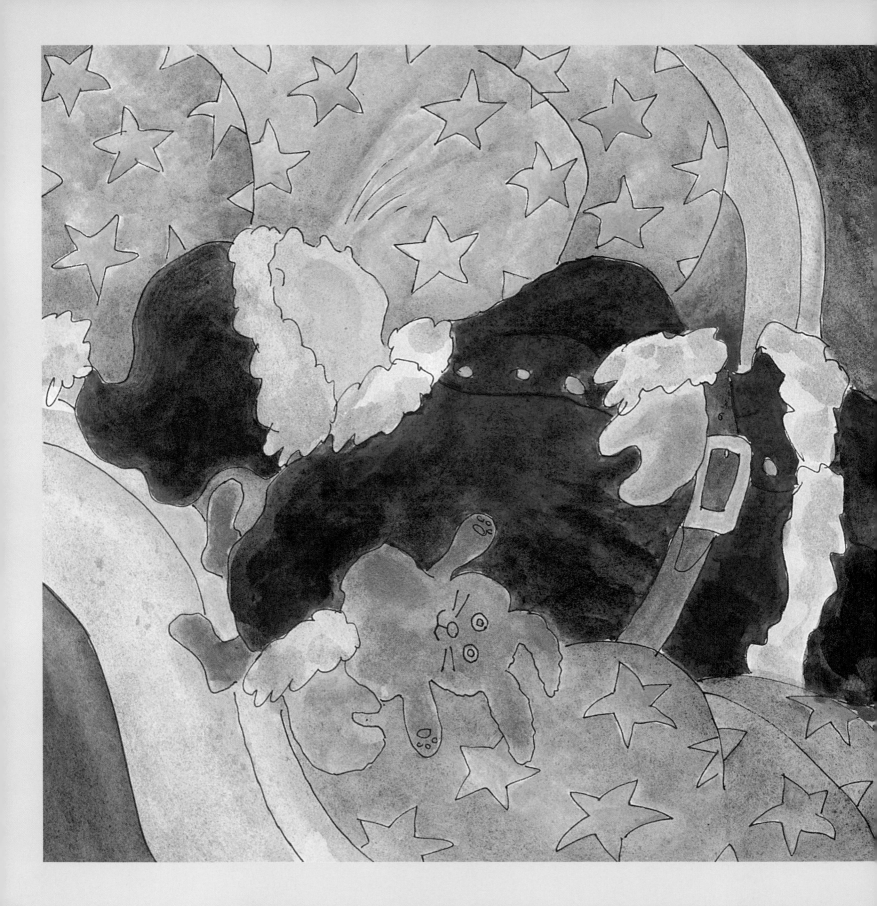

Rodney did not know what to do.
If Santa didn't wake up, kids all over the world
would be very disappointed.
And Santa would not wake up, even when
Rodney growled at him!

At the next house Rodney borrowed Santa's hat and went to work filling stockings. He did the best he could, but he was only a dog.

He couldn't just zip up the chimney like Santa. He had to sort of scramble up with the heavy bag in his teeth.

It
was
hard.

At the end of the night, the job was finally done, and they flew home.
Rodney was dog tired. For some unknown reason, so was Santa.
"Rough night," said Santa.
"RUFF!" said Rodney.
They both shuffled off to dognap on the couch.

The elves knew Rodney had saved the day.
They began calling him "Santa Paws."
But the next week the complaint
letters started coming in.

"This has got to change!" cried the head elf.
He's sure right about that, thought Rodney.
He was watching TV with Santa.
There was a commercial for a self-help video called
Take Charge of Your Life!
"In just ten easy lessons you can get your act together!"
said the announcer. "Send for the video today!"

So Rodney did.
He was a good dog.

Rodney got his act together in a big way! He took charge!
He learned to speak and read seven languages!
His new computer skills straightened out all the toy orders.
The whole toy workshop was humming and efficient.

CLAUS AND PAWS, INC.

ONLY 2 6 0 DAYS UNTIL CHRISTMAS!

But Santa was still a major slacker.

Rodney took charge again!
He knew he would have to teach Santa how to live up to his name.

1. Rodney turned off the TV.

2. He read inspiring Christmas books to Santa.

The Mouses Terrible Christmas

3. He gave Santa pep talks.

TIPS:
1. Be Merry!
2. Use the Ho Ho Ho
3. Eat more cookies
4. U

That's how Santa learned to be the hardworking spirit of Christmas we know today!

¡Feliz Navidad!

Ho Ho Ho MERRY CHRISTMAS!

Good dog, Rodney!

Rodney later took charge of that
lazy, good-for-nothing Easter Bunny.

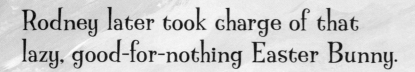